MR. MEN LITTLE MISS™

Mr. NOISY'S WILD SAFARI

Turn to page 32 to find out what the pictures mean!

THE MR. MEN SHOW® and DILLYDALE® copyright © 2009 THOIP (a Chorion company). All rights reserved. Published by Price Stern Sloan, a division of Penguin Young Readers Group, 345 Hudson Street, New York, New York 10014. *PSS!* is a registered trademark of Penguin Group (USA) Inc. Printed in the U.S.A.

www.mrmen.com

PSS!
PRICE STERN SLOAN
www.penguin.com/youngreaders

The publisher does not have any control over and does not assume any responsibility for author or third-party websites or their content.

ISBN 978-0-8431-3572-5   10 9 8 7 6 5 4 3 2 1

 and had

been looking for

all day. But so far

all they had was

a of 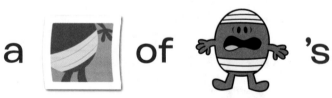's

rear end!

"Maybe the would

come if you weren't so

noisy," said .

"Nonsense," said .

"All we need is my

secret weapon: the

Finicky Panpipe!"

Just then, **3**   landed on the  branch.

"Whoa!"  cried.

"That's great!" shouted

 . "Where's my

 ?"

"Poopity poop!"

yelled  .

The had flown

away and poopity-

pooped on his head!

"What a great  ,"

said  . "Say  !"

aimed his

at . "You're not

smiling," said .

"I wonder why not,"

grumbled .

"Let's move on to our

next animal," said .

11

Next, wanted

to get a of the

great  .

"The great  is

very big," said  .

"Can we take a

of a instead?"

"No way! We need

a !" shouted  .

"And I know just how to

find one. We'll use my

secret secret weapon:

the **2**-Tone Bamboo

 Bagpipe!"

"Too bad," said  .

"Looks like the

didn't work!"

Just then, the great

 sat on top of him.

"Poopity poop!"

cried  .

"Another great !"

said  . "Say  !"

"I can't," moaned .

"I was talking to the

 ," replied .

Next, wanted

to find an  .

"And not just any

 ," said 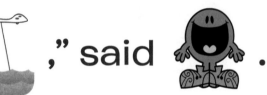 .

"I want to find the

rare great white

 !"

" ?" said . "You

didn't say we were

looking for **1** of those."

"I'll just use my secret

secret secret weapon:

the All-Aluminum

Whistle," said .

began to play

his .

"Ummm, ?" said

 .

" !" yelled

as the  opened

its mouth.

"Quiet down, .

You'll scare the

away," said .

He played his

again.

"Yuck!" said the  .

He spit out  ,

who tasted very bad!

"Poopity poop!"

said  .

"I guess my didn't

work," said .

"  ? Where did you go?" said .

"Oh, well. I guess I'll have to find the hungry horn-tailed hippo on my own!"

Read along with these words.

Mr. Bump

Mr. Noisy

flamingos

picture

three

tree

camera

cheese

buffalo

squirrel

two

bagpipe

alligator

one

whistle